DC SUPER HEROES

BATMAN™

AND THE

MISSING PUNCHLINE

WRITTEN BY
MICHAEL ANTHONY STEELE

ILLUSTRATED BY
GREGG SCHIGIEL

BATMAN CREATED BY
BOB KANE WITH BILL FINGER

Raintree is an imprint of Capstone Global Library Limited, a company incorporated
in England and Wales having its registered office at 264 Banbury Road, Oxford, OX2
7DY – Registered company number: 6695582
www.raintree.co.uk
myorders@raintree.co.uk

Designed by Brann Garvey

978 1 3982 0608 3

British Library Cataloguing in Publication Data
A full catalogue record for this book is available from the British Library.

Printed and bound in the United Kingdom

CONTENTS

While still a boy, Bruce Wayne witnessed the death of his parents at the hands of a petty criminal. The tragic event changed the young billionaire's life forever. Bruce vowed to rid Gotham City of evil and keep its people safe from crime. After years of training his body and mind, he donned a new uniform and a new identity.

He became . . .

CHAPTER I

Batwoman to the rescue

"Bruce Wayne!" squealed the woman in the sparkling evening gown. "It's been so long since we've seen you out on the town, darling."

Bruce choked on his drink in surprise. He was careful not to spill any on his tuxedo. "Oh, hi," Bruce said. "It's good to see you again . . . uh . . ."

"Elaine Winthrop, you silly goose," the woman finished for him.

"Yes, of course." Bruce chuckled. He fumbled with his glass and snack plate before taking the woman's outstretched hand. "Wonderful to see you, Mrs Winthrop."

The woman laughed and gave him a playful pat on the shoulder. "I don't see how you run a huge company with that memory of yours."

"Sorry." Bruce shrugged. "I've been working a lot of nights."

That wasn't a lie. Bruce Wayne normally spent his evenings fighting crime in Gotham City as Batman. But every now and then, multibillionaire Bruce Wayne had to appear at a charity ball such as this one.

"Well, no work tonight, Bruce," said Mrs Winthrop. "Tonight is about having fun!" She touched her diamond necklace. "And maybe showing off some new jewellery."

"And it's for a good cause," Bruce said. He pointed to the large banner draped across the ballroom. It read: *Save the Gotham City Animal Shelters.*

"Oh, that too," said Mrs Winthrop. "Now, come, Bruce. I must introduce you to some friends of mine."

"Maybe in a moment," Bruce said as he scanned the crowd of wealthy guests. He spotted a woman wearing black trousers and a sparkling jacket. She had short red hair and gave a smile when they locked eyes.

"Well, don't be too long," Mrs Winthrop said with a wave. She disappeared back into the crowd.

When Bruce was alone, the short-haired woman glided up to him. She was Bruce's cousin, Kate Kane.

"Have you tried the crab cakes?" Bruce asked her. "They're delicious." He popped one into his mouth.

"None for me, thanks," said Kate. "I won't be here long. I'm about to go on patrol." Kate Kane also fought crime in Gotham City – as Batwoman.

"Same here," Bruce said between bites. "But . . . since Wayne Industries sponsored this event, I should stick around a bit longer."

Kate laughed and brushed a crumb off his tuxedo jacket. "You certainly play the part of the clueless billionaire well."

Bruce shrugged and smiled. "Who says it's an act?"

Kate shook her head. "You and I know better." She turned to leave. "See you out there." She disappeared into the crowd.

Bruce felt more relaxed than he had in a long time. His butler, Alfred Pennyworth, had always encouraged him to take more time off from being Batman. Perhaps Alfred was right. Maybe he should take more breaks from fighting crime. This evening was turning out to be just what the butler had in mind.

Bruce finished his drink and placed his empty plate and glass on the tray of a passing server. The men and women in white coats milled through the crowd offering food and drinks to the elegant guests.

KRASH!

All the servers dropped their trays at once. They each reached into their jackets and pulled out black batons. Electricity crackled from the ends of the rods as they held them up high.

"All right, everyone," one of the servers shouted. "This is a robbery!"

"Any of you fat cats make a move," bellowed another server, "and we'll shock every last one of you!"

Oddly enough, the guests seemed delighted by the display of force. Some even clapped, as if they were watching some kind of performance.

"Was this your doing, Bruce?" Mrs Winthrop asked as she slid in next to him. She grinned. "What a wonderful show!"

Something in the back of Bruce's mind told him he should do something about this crime. But just like the others, he felt lightly amused by the situation.

"All right, let's have it," said a server with a large white bag.

Another server moved in with her own bag. "Jewellery, wallets . . . in the bags. Now!"

The guests chuckled while they did as they were told. The women dropped in necklaces, bracelets and handbags. The men slid off watches and pulled out their wallets. No one seemed concerned about being robbed.

Bruce slid off his own watch and pulled out his wallet. Unlike the other guests, he knew this wasn't a performance. He had seen enough crime to know that this was the real thing. Unfortunately, he didn't feel the urge to do anything about it. Something kept him cheerful about the whole thing.

BAM!

Two side doors burst open and a dark figure stood in the doorway. The figure wore all black and had a flowing cape. Two short points jutted out from the figure's head.

"Is . . . is that . . . Batman?" asked one of the crooks.

"Guess again," said the mysterious figure. She leapt over the crowd, flipped in mid-air, and came down on the crook with both boots. He dropped the electrified baton as he tumbled across the floor.

"Batwoman!" cried another criminal. "Get her!"

The robbers dropped their bags of loot and ran towards the crime-fighter. Sparks of electricity jumped from the ends of their batons as they swung them at Batwoman. She ducked under one baton before delivering a spinning kick to her attacker.

Batwoman blocked two more attacks before dealing a series of punches to three of the criminals. They were out before they hit the floor.

Something about seeing Batwoman in action helped Bruce fight whatever strange spell he was under. He shook his head to clear it before edging towards the battle. He couldn't join the fight the way he would if he were Batman. But he had to help somehow.

As Batwoman fought the criminals, two of the servers sneaked up behind her. Their batons sparked as they prepared to shock the crime-fighter in the back.

Bruce pretended to trip and stumble. "Excuse me," he said as he slammed into one of the attackers. That crook tottered forwards and shocked the other robber. The man crumpled to the floor, unconscious.

The criminal that Bruce had banged into spun around. "I'll get you for that!" she growled as she jabbed at the billionaire with the sparkling baton.

"I'm sorry," said Bruce as he dodged the attack. "It was an accident."

"Let's see if you like *this* accident," the crook said as she pushed forward. She swung her baton, driving Bruce back towards the nearby balcony. When Bruce's back was to the railing, he glanced over the edge. They were ten storeys up.

The crook snarled as she raised her baton over her head. She charged forward and swung recklessly at the billionaire. Bruce ducked at the last minute, and the robber flipped over the railing.

Without thinking, Bruce reached over the side and grabbed the criminal's arm. Unfortunately, the weight of the crook dragged Bruce over the edge. Batman had enough equipment to take a dive like that, but not Bruce Wayne.

Luckily, Bruce heard a familiar sound behind him.

POW!

It was the sound of a grapnel being fired.

Bruce held tight to the crook's arm as he felt a thin cable wrap around one of his ankles. The cable pulled tight and they stopped falling. As he and the crook swayed from side to side, Bruce looked back up at the balcony.

Batwoman looked down at him. She had saved their lives.

CHAPTER 2

The missing punchline

"And here I thought you would have at least one night off," Alfred Pennyworth said as he put down a breakfast tray on the computer console in the Batcave.

"No such luck," said Batwoman. She and Batman sat at the Batcomputer. They stared up at the main monitor. Lines of data streamed across the screen.

"There must have been something mixed in with the food and drink from last night," Batman said as he typed on the keyboard.

"It makes sense," Batwoman agreed. "I didn't eat or drink anything last night, so I wasn't affected."

"And I was," said Batman. He had finally stopped feeling the effects of whatever had made him amused by the robbery.

"I'm assuming you brought back samples of the tainted refreshments?" asked Alfred.

"The computer's analysing them now," replied Batman. "It may take a while, but if there's something there, it will find it."

Alfred stepped forward and pointed to one of the smaller computer screens. It showed a woman who appeared to be filming herself for social media.

"Since you insist on monitoring all of Gotham City's activities," the butler said, "perhaps you should focus on this young lady's video."

Batman tapped a few keys and the image of the woman filled the main screen. The video's sound flowed from the speakers.

"Can you believe it?" the woman asked. "The bank's being robbed. How cool is that?" She waved and smiled as crooks wearing gas masks hurried about in the background.

Batman checked another screen. "No alarms were triggered. The police have no idea this is happening."

"And she doesn't seem too worried about the situation," Batwoman noted.

"Yes," agreed Batman. "Sound familiar?"

The two crime-fighters sprinted towards

the waiting Batmobile. They leapt into the open hatch and the engine roared to life. The hatch slid shut as the vehicle rocketed out of the Batcave.

Alfred sighed and picked up the untouched breakfast tray. "And I suppose you won't have the morning off, either."

* * *

"Come on!" shouted one of the bank robbers. His voice was muffled through his gas mask. "This is taking too long."

"What's the rush?" asked another masked criminal. "No one hit any alarm buttons." He pointed at the group of customers and bank employees sitting along a wall. "Look at 'em! They don't even care that they're being robbed."

The group of people simply smiled back at

him. A couple even waved.

The first robber held up the small metal canister. "They won't be like that for much longer. We're almost out of gas."

"All right," said a third robber as he hauled a large bag over his shoulder. "We've got enough. Let's get out of here!"

All five masked criminals ran towards the main doors. Just as they were about to exit, something sent them flying backwards. Cash fluttered into the air as the crooks tumbled across the floor. As they scrambled to their feet, the robbers saw that their exit was blocked – by Batman and Batwoman.

"I would recommend you give yourselves up," Batwoman said, her voice muffled by her own gas mask. "But where's the fun in that?" The crime-fighters charged at the crooks.

Wearing a small gas mask of his own, Batman closed in on the nearest robber. He held up an arm as the thug swung a bag of cash at him.

SLASH!

The points on the Dark Knight's glove cut through the bag and all the money spilled out. The criminal was left holding an empty sack as Batman dropped and kicked the crook's legs out from under him. **THUD!** The crook hit the floor, and the crime-fighter moved on to the next robber.

Batwoman leapt into the air, flipped over one robber and landed between two more. **POW!** She punched one, sending him staggering back. Then she ducked as the other crook took a swing at her. She spun around, landing a kick to his chest. **WHACK!** He slammed against a wall – out cold.

The robber with the metal canister sneaked up behind Batwoman as she fought. He raised it above his head, ready to strike.

WHIP·PANG!

Batman fired his grapnel at the canister and it clamped on. The Dark Knight jerked the line and the canister flew from the crook's hands. Batman swung the canister around and slammed it into the surprised criminal, knocking him out.

Meanwhile, Batwoman ducked and dodged swings from the other two robbers. "All right," she said. "Enough messing around." She grabbed both by the back of the neck and slammed them into each other.

SMACK!

Both robbers fell to the ground in an unconscious heap.

The crime-fighters slowly turned around as the bank customers and employees applauded. A couple even cheered and whistled.

"And I thought this was a thankless job," said Batwoman.

Batman looked at the canister in his hand and shook his head.

CHAPTER 3

No laughing matter

Batman jerked the steering wheel as the Batmobile darted through Gotham City traffic. Batwoman was strapped into the passenger seat.

"That was a familiar scene, wasn't it?" she asked.

"All too familiar," Batman replied. He nodded at the small green canister in her lap. "And I think that might be the key."

"Too bad none of the crooks would say who gave it to them," Batwoman added.

The Dark Knight pressed a button on the console and a view screen snapped to life. Alfred Pennyworth's face appeared.

"Alfred, has the computer finished analysing the food and drink samples from last night?" Batman asked.

"Yes," replied the butler. "And I don't think you'll be happy with the results."

Batman scowled. "What was in them?"

"Traces of Joker toxin, sir," Alfred replied.

"Joker toxin?" asked Batwoman. "That's some strong stuff."

The Joker was one of Batman's most dangerous enemies. His deadly toxin left his victims laughing out of control with freakish grins stretched across their faces.

Batman swerved around a large truck. "True. But maybe in small doses it just makes its victims amused and obedient." He shook his head. "That's how it made me feel."

The Caped Crusader pressed another button and a small hatch in the Batmobile opened. A thin plastic tube uncoiled from the compartment.

"Alfred, connect the Batcomputer to the Batmobile's onboard computer. Compare this new sample to your results."

Batwoman attached the end of the tube to the connection port on the green canister. She slowly opened the port's valve, releasing a tiny bit of the gas into the tube.

"Analysing," said the butler. He paused for a moment, then reported, "An exact match, sir."

"That makes sense," said Batman. Then he shook his head. "But something's off. This isn't the Joker's style. It's just plain robbery. There's no joke . . . no punchline."

"And isn't he still locked up in Arkham Asylum?" asked Batwoman.

"He's supposed to be," Batman said before jerking the wheel to one side. The Batmobile skidded around a corner and roared down a side street. "I'd like to see for myself."

"Maybe I should track down some of his former henchmen," Batwoman suggested. "See if they have something to do with the watered-down toxin."

"Good idea," Batman agreed. He pressed a button on his steering wheel and the main hatch slid open. "Let me know what you find out."

Batwoman unbuckled herself and raised her grapnel into the air. She shot the hook at a passing building. When the hook locked onto the structure, she was jerked out of the Batmobile. The cable tightened and she swung towards the rooftops.

Once she was gone, Batman closed the hatch. His hands tightened on the wheel as he sped towards Arkham Asylum.

In no time, the Batmobile pulled through the iron gate and skidded to a stop in front of the towering building. The hatch slid open and Batman leapt out, his long cape flowing behind him.

The Dark Knight entered the asylum and marched towards the nearest orderly. "I need to see the Joker, now."

The thin man in a blue shirt nervously led the way through the dark corridors.

"I don't know if you'll get anything out of him, Mr Batman, sir," the orderly croaked. "He's been in one of his moods."

The crime-fighter's eyes narrowed. "What do you mean?"

"He won't eat or even talk to anyone," the orderly replied, glancing up tentatively at the Dark Knight. "He just sits in his cell telling one joke after another. He's been like that all day."

Batman's lips tightened. Perhaps the orderly was right. When the Clown Prince of Crime was in one of his dark moods, he made even less sense than usual. He might not give up any information about his toxin after all.

When they reached his cell block, Batman could hear the Joker's crazed voice from several cells away.

"Why is a football stadium so hot after a game?" the Joker asked. "Because all the fans have left!" He burst into insane laughter.

Batman marched up to the cell and peeked through a small window in the iron door. He could just make out the form of the criminal sitting in a dark corner of his cell.

"We need to talk, Joker," the Dark Knight barked.

"Why did the short ghost join the football team?" asked the Joker. He didn't wait for a reply. "Because they needed a little team spirit!" More crazed laughter.

"Oh, yeah. And they're all American football jokes for some reason," the orderly added. "I've heard this one a dozen times."

"Because they needed a little team spirit!" the Joker repeated before cackling with laughter.

Batman turned to the orderly. "The Joker doesn't repeat jokes," he growled. "He can't stand repeating jokes."

"What can I say?" The orderly shrugged. "He's been doing it all day."

"Open the cell door," Batman said through gritted teeth.

"Are you sure that's such a good –" the orderly began.

"Now!" Batman interrupted.

The man fumbled with a ring of keys before finally finding the right one. His hand shook as he jabbed the key into the keyhole.

CLANK! The lock echoed down the corridor as the orderly turned the key.

The Caped Crusader shoved past the orderly and swung open the door. He swooped into the cell and lunged for the

Joker. He pulled the figure into the light only to discover that . . . it was a dummy. Its grinning face looked exactly like the Joker's as it stared back at the crime-fighter. A small digital recorder hung around the dummy's neck.

"Why can't you play football in the jungle?" asked the Joker's voice from the recorder. "Because there are too many cheetahs!" The voice roared with laughter again.

Batman growled with anger. The Joker had escaped.

CHAPTER 4

Black market bust

Batwoman perched on a rooftop high above Gotham City. She had tracked down a few of the Joker's former henchmen, but they knew nothing about the weak toxin. Now, she was trying one last thing to help solve this mystery.

The crime-fighter focused her binoculars on the scene below. Several people milled around the various cars and trucks parked in the dark alley.

This wasn't a random gathering. It was a mobile black market swap meet. Here one could buy stolen goods, weapons, almost anything.

Both she and Batman had busted it several times. But no matter how many times they took it down, the crooks always seemed to find a way to organize it again. If someone was selling watered-down Joker toxin, this would be the place to do it.

She scanned the milling crowd of criminals. It was a long shot, but maybe, just maybe, she could spot . . .

Batwoman shifted her focus to a pair of crooks in the shadows. A man pulled out a wad of cash and handed it to a figure in a hooded trench coat. The cloaked figure took the cash and then produced a small green gas canister.

"Got you," Batwoman said as she put her binoculars away. She dived off the rooftop and rocketed towards the scene below. Then, at the last minute, she spread her cape wide. She caught enough air to slow her down before landing in the middle of the marketplace.

"We're busted!" someone shouted as truck engines roared to life. Crooks scattered and vehicles pulled away.

Normally, Batwoman would've tried to take down as many of the criminals as possible. But right now, she only had eyes for two of them. The trouble was that they were running in two different directions.

Batwoman needed to chase the criminal in the trench coat. But she also didn't want the canister of Joker toxin to be used in another crime.

The hero reached into her Utility Belt and pulled out a small tracker. She hurled it down the alley and it stuck to the back of the trench coat. The tracker's red light blinked as the crook disappeared around a corner.

Batwoman ran after the man with the canister and tackled him. She wrenched the canister from him as he stood up to fight.

"Hey, I paid good money for that," he said as he picked up a nearby pipe.

The ten criminals who hadn't escaped began closing in. They picked up boards and chains, ready to attack. Batwoman was surrounded.

"I don't have time for this," Batwoman growled. She knew she could take them all. But the person in the trench coat was getting further and further away. She had to find out who was behind the Joker toxin.

The crime-fighter reached into her Utility Belt and pulled out her small gas mask. She put it on and opened the valve of the canister.

HISSSSS!

Green gas sprayed out of the canister and flooded the alley.

"I'll tell you what," Batwoman said. "Why don't you all just sit down against that wall and take a break. You can wait for the police."

The crooks glanced at each other before dropping their weapons and moving towards the wall.

"That sounds like a great idea," one of them said with a grin.

Another criminal clapped his hands with excitement. "We get to ride in a police car! Oooh, I hope they put the siren on!"

Once everyone was sitting peacefully, Batwoman put down the emptying canister and pulled out her grapnel. She fired it at a nearby rooftop and it pulled her off the ground and into the night.

The crime-fighter ran across rooftops and leapt from building to building. She held a small device in one hand, following the tiny red blip on the screen. The tracker led her to a warehouse several blocks over.

SWISH!

Batwoman swung onto the roof and gazed in through a large skylight.

A door opened in the room below and the cloaked figure entered. The figure dropped the trench coat, revealing a woman wearing a black and red body suit. Her face was painted white and a jester's hat sat on top of her head.

"Harley Quinn," Batwoman said with a snarl. She jumped forward and crashed through the skylight. She dropped to the floor in a shower of glass.

Harley gasped with surprise. "I knew I had bats in my belfry," she said. "But this is ridiculous!"

The criminal ran across the room and grabbed an oversized mallet. She grunted as she swung it at Batwoman's head. The crime-fighter ducked the blow and then landed a kick to Harley's stomach.

"Ooof!" Harley said as she dropped the mallet.

Batwoman picked it up and broke the handle over her knee. "Why are you selling Joker toxin, Harley?" she asked. "Where's the joke in letting other crooks use it?"

"Oh, there's no joke, sweetheart," Harley replied before back-flipping across the room. She landed beside a closed door. "I just needed some cash. After all, someone has to pay the food bill while Mr J is locked away." She opened the door. "Crackers! Giggles! Mama's got company!"

Two giant hyenas burst from the room. They cackled with laughter as they charged at Batwoman.

The crime-fighter was able to dodge the first beast, but the second one pushed her to the floor. She pressed her forearm against its neck, barely holding back its snapping jaws.

Batwoman pushed off the floor and flipped the animal over her head. She sprang to her feet and then leapt out of the way as the first hyena lunged at her. She landed on top of a stack of crates.

Batwoman dug through her Utility Belt. She pulled out a set of bolas and hurled them at one of the animals. The hard balls at the end of three ropes wrapped around the beast's legs and it hit the floor.

"Crackers!" Harley shouted.

Batwoman leapt clear as Giggles bounded towards her. He crashed through a crate and its contents flew everywhere. The crate was full of hot dog buns.

The crime-fighter reached back into her belt and grabbed another weapon. She whipped her hand towards the other hyena and a large net flew through the air. It wrapped around the beast, trapping it.

"Giggles!" Harley shouted. She reached into a nearby cupboard, pulled out another mallet, and charged. "Don't worry, darlings! Mama's comin'!"

Batwoman caught the handle of the mallet just as Harley brought it down. The two struggled for control of the weapon.

"Who else did you sell toxin to, Harley?" asked Batwoman.

"Oh, that watered-down stuff?" Harley asked. She laughed as she strained against the crime-fighter's hold. "No one else. We need the rest for the biggest joke of all!"

Batwoman's eyes widened. "We?"

Suddenly, a boxing glove came out of nowhere and slammed against Batwoman's head. She crumpled to the floor, out cold.

The Joker smiled as he reeled in the glove. "And you won't believe the punchline." He roared with laughter.

CHAPTER 5

Free refreshments

Batman dropped through the broken skylight. Bits of glass crunched beneath his boots as he moved about the room. A red light blinked on the tiny screen in his hand, leading him to the trench coat on the floor. He reached down and pulled off the tiny tracker.

The Dark Knight touched the side of his head. "Any word from Batwoman, Penny-One?" he asked. Penny-One was Alfred's code name.

"Nothing yet, sir, I'm afraid," replied the butler's voice in his earpiece.

The World's Greatest Detective pulled out a torch and began scanning the room for clues. The first thing he spotted was an oversized mallet – the handle snapped in half. Batman sneered. "Harley Quinn."

He then spotted the net and set of bolas on the floor. Many of their ropes had been sliced apart. Batman moved the torch beam onto a smashed crate.

Hot dog buns? Batman thought. *What are you up to, Joker?*

The Dark Knight scanned the room for more clues. He spotted an American football helmet, cheerleading pom-poms and a jersey for Gotham City's American football team – the Gotham Knights.

"Hmm . . . I think I know the Joker's next target," the Caped Crusader told Alfred. "I need to get to Gotham City Stadium as quickly as possible."

"The Batmobile is not fast enough for you, sir?" Alfred asked.

Batman pressed a button on his Utility Belt. "I'm sending the Batmobile back," he said. "I'll need something faster."

Alfred paused a moment, then said, "It's on its way."

* * *

Once again, Batwoman struggled against the ropes that held her tight. But just as before, the hyenas on either side of her turned and growled. They bared their sharp teeth until she stopped moving. She wasn't going anywhere.

The crime-fighter was tied up in front of a small stage at the centre of the Gotham Knights' American football field. Football fans filled the stadium around her, but they didn't seem to care that she was trapped between two vicious animals.

"Looks like everyone's been dosed with more watered-down Joker toxin," Batwoman murmured.

"You better believe it," the Joker said as he hopped onto the stage. He snatched the microphone from the stand and looked up at the crowd. "Is everyone ready for the half-time show?"

The audience cheered in response.

The Joker chuckled. "I see everyone has enjoyed the free refreshments we provided."

The audience cheered louder.

"Good, good," the Joker said. "Now, I've been working on some new material just for this occasion." The criminal cleared his throat. "Why did they kick Cinderella off the football team?"

"Why?" the audience asked in unison.

"Because she kept running away from the ball," the Joker said, bursting into laughter.

The obedient audience laughed along with him.

Harley Quinn flipped up on stage. She shook two black and red pom-poms. "Joker! Joker! He's our man!" she cheered. "If he can't make you laugh, no one can!"

"Not now, Harley," the Joker growled. "Save it for the big finish."

Harley froze and hung her head. "Sorry, Mr J," she said.

The Joker turned back towards the crowd. "That's right, folks," he said with a grin. "After a quick game of Splat the Bat . . ." Harley grinned and pointed to the giant mallet on the stage. "The grand finale will be fireworks containing my *full-strength* Joker toxin!" The Joker laughed and then covered his mouth. "Whoops! Spoiler alert!"

Once again, the audience didn't seem to mind the threat. They cheered even louder.

Suddenly, a dark shadow covered the stadium. The Batplane hovered in the sky before landing on the football field.

"Oh, boy," the Joker moaned. "Don't you just hate hecklers?"

Harley broke out into another cheer. "Two, four, six, eight! Who do we annihilate? Batman! Batman! Yay!"

The plane's hatch slid open and Batman sprang from the cockpit. He flipped in mid-air before landing in front of the small stage.

"We got this, Mr J," Harley said as she dropped her pom-poms. She grabbed her mallet and pointed at Batman. "Crackers! Giggles! Fetch!"

The hyenas tore after the Dark Knight. Batman didn't run. Instead, he reached into his Utility Belt and flung two tranquilizer darts at the beasts. They struck the animals and knocked them out cold. The hyenas slid to a stop at Batman's feet.

Harley frowned and stomped a foot. "Hey, not fair!"

With the hyenas out of the picture, Batwoman pulled a Batarang from her Utility Belt. She used its sharp edge to cut through her ropes.

In a flash, Batwoman was on her feet and on the move. She kicked Harley Quinn as the crook raised her mallet. The criminal flew back several metres.

The Joker growled in frustration. "Must I do everything myself?!!" He grabbed the microphone stand and charged at Batman.

The audience cheered as the battle began. The Joker swung at Batman with the stand while Harley Quinn swung at Batwoman with the mallet. The two crime-fighters easily dodged the attacks.

Batwoman moved in before Harley could raise the mallet again.

BAM! BAM! BAM! SMACK!

She performed three quick punches and a spinning kick before the criminal knew what hit her.

Harley dropped the mallet and crumpled to the ground.

Meanwhile, Batman blocked another blow from the Joker. The Dark Knight grabbed the stand and wrestled it from the crook's hands. But as he gave up his weapon, the Joker landed several punches on the Caped Crusader. Batman stumbled back, then tossed the mic stand aside.

The Joker shook his head and sighed. "You really do ruin everything, don't you?" He pulled out a small remote and pressed a red button. "So much for my big finish."

POW·POW·POW·POW! POW!

Fireworks launched all around them. They shot into the air and exploded into bright-green clouds of gas. The clouds began to drift towards the crowd.

"Oooh!" shouted the unaware audience all around the stadium. "Ah!"

"Batman! Those fireworks are full of Joker toxin," Batwoman explained. "And it's at *full* strength!"

Batman growled and punched the Joker. Then the crime-fighter touched the side of his head.

"Penny-One, take control of the Batplane," the Dark Knight commanded.

"At once, sir," replied Alfred's voice in Batman's earpiece. The plane's engines fired up, and the jet rose off the field.

"We have some air pollution here," Batman said as he blocked another attack from the Joker.

"Ah, yes," Alfred replied. "I see it."

The Batplane hovered over the stadium. A hatch on the belly of the plane slid open and a large hose snaked out. As the plane circled the stadium, its large hose sucked up the toxic green gas.

"Good job," Batman said. He cuffed the Joker's hands behind his back.

"A butler does know how to vacuum," Alfred replied.

Once the air was clear, the hose retracted and the plane levelled out. It buzzed over the football field.

WHOOOSH!

Batman's cape fluttered as the jet raced by. The unsuspecting football fans cheered at the dazzling air show.

The Joker wobbled on his feet, watching the Batplane. "Well, that wasn't very funny."

Batwoman dragged over a cuffed and groggy Harley Quinn. "Looks like the joke's on you two," she said.

Batman walked the Joker off the field. "And the punchline is there's no escape for you this time."

The Joker flashed his wicked grin. "We'll just see about that," he murmured.

The
Joker

REAL NAME: Unknown

OCCUPATION: Professional Criminal

HEIGHT: 2 metres

WEIGHT: 87 kg

EYES: Green

HAIR: Green

POWERS/ABILITIES: Genius-level intelligence, chemistry and engineering skills

BIOGRAPHY:
The Clown Prince of Crime. The Ace of Knaves. Batman's most dangerous enemy is known by many names, but he answers to no one. After falling into a vat of toxic waste, this once lowly criminal was transformed into an evil madman. The chemical bath bleached his skin, dyed his hair green, and peeled back his lips into a permanent grin. Since then, the Joker has only one purpose in life: to destroy Batman. In the meantime, he's happy tormenting the people of Gotham City.

- The Joker always wants the last laugh. To get it, he's devised dozens of deadly clown tricks. He has even gone so far as faking his own death.

- Always the trickster, the Joker designs all of his weapons to look comical in order to conceal their true danger. This trickery usually gets a chuckle or two from his foes, giving the Joker an opportunity to strike first.

- The Clown Prince of Crime has spent more time in Arkham Asylum than any Gotham City criminal. But that doesn't mean he's comfortable behind bars. He has also escaped more times than anyone.

- While at Arkham, the Joker met Dr Harleen Quinzel. She fell in love with the crazy clown and aided in his many escapes. Soon, she turned to a life of crime herself, as the evil jester Harley Quinn.

BIOGRAPHIES

AUTHOR

Michael Anthony Steele has been in the entertainment industry for more than 27 years, writing for television, movies and video games. He has authored more than 120 books for exciting characters and brands, including Batman, Superman, Wonder Woman, Spider-Man, Shrek, Scooby-Doo, LEGO City, Garfield, *Winx Club, Night at the Museum* and *The Penguins of Madagascar*. Mr Steele lives on a ranch in Texas, USA, but he enjoys meeting his readers when he visits schools and libraries all across the United States. For more information, visit MichaelAnthonySteele.com.

Illustrator

Cartoonist **Gregg Schigiel** is the creator / author / illustrator of the superhero / fairy tale mash-up Pix graphic novels and was a regular contributor to Spongebob Comics. Outside of work, Mr Schigiel bakes prize-winning cookies, enjoys comedy and makes sure he drinks plenty of water. Learn more at greggschigiel.com.

GLOSSARY

analyse to examine something carefully in order to understand it

asylum a hospital for people who are mentally ill

bola a weapon made of several balls connected to a rope that is thrown to entangle prey

charity a group that raises money or collects goods to help people or animals in need

grapnel a grappling hook connected to a rope that can be fired like a gun

hyena a large, doglike animal that lives in Africa and Asia

obedient willing to follow rules and commands

toxin a poisonous substance produced by a living thing

tranquilizer   a drug that has a calming effect

unconscious not aware; not able to see, feel or think

DISCUSSION QUESTIONS

1. Why did Batman need both Batwoman and Alfred to help him defeat the Joker and Harley Quinn in this story? What might have happened if one or both of his allies hadn't been able to help?

2. Batman discovers a dummy of the Joker repeating jokes at Arkham Asylum. What was the theme of these jokes? What clues do they provide Batman about the Joker's plans?

3. Batman and Batwoman don't have superpowers, but they still find ways to defeat their foes. What skills make them so successful in their fight against crime?

WRITING PROMPTS

1. Batman and Batwoman use a lot of gadgets to fight crime. If you could have your own crime-fighting gadget, what would it be? Write a paragraph describing your gadget and how it would work.

2. Harley Quinn and Batwoman are pretty evenly matched in their battles. Who would win if they fought again? Write a short story about their next encounter that shows who gets the upper hand!

3. At the end of the story, the Joker hints at having plans to escape once again. Write another chapter that explains how he and Harley Quinn get away!

LOOK FOR MORE

DC SUPER HERO ADVENTURES